P9-DHT-781

NOBODY'S PERFECT.
I'M AS CLOSE AS IT GETS.

THINK YOU CAN HANDLE
JAMIE KELLY'S FIRST YEAR OF DIARIES?

AND DON'T MISS YEAR TWO!

DEAR DUMB DIARY,

YEAR TWO

NOBODY'S PERFECT. I'M AS CLOSE AS IT GETS.

BY JAMIE KELLY

SCHOLASTIC INC.

ISBN 978-0-545-37764-5

Copyright © 2013 by Jim Benton

All rights reserved. Published by Scholastic Inc.
SCHOLASTIC and associated logos are trademarks
and/or registered trademarks of Scholastic Inc.
DEAR DUMB DIARY is a registered trademark of Jim Benton.

12 11 10 9 8 7 6 5 4 3 2   13 14 15 16 17/0
Printed in the U.S.A.   40
First printing, January 2013

For Griffin, Summer, and Mary K.

Thanks to Shannon Penney, Jackie Hornberger, Yaffa Jaskoll, Anna Bloom, and Kristen LeClerc, all of whom would be willing to tell you just how perfect they are.

HEY

WANT TO HAVE AN AWESOME FUTURE?

WELL,

Stop Reading my Diary

OR

You won't have any FUTURE

AT ALL

THIS DIARY
-PROPERTY OF-

Jamie Kelly

SCHOOL: _MACKEREL MIDDLE SCHOOL_

EXTRACURRICULARS: _UM..._

FUTURE PLANS: _I don't really know...um..._

COLLEGE GOALS: _I DON'T KNOW_
LET'S TALK ABOUT
SOMETHING ELSE NOW

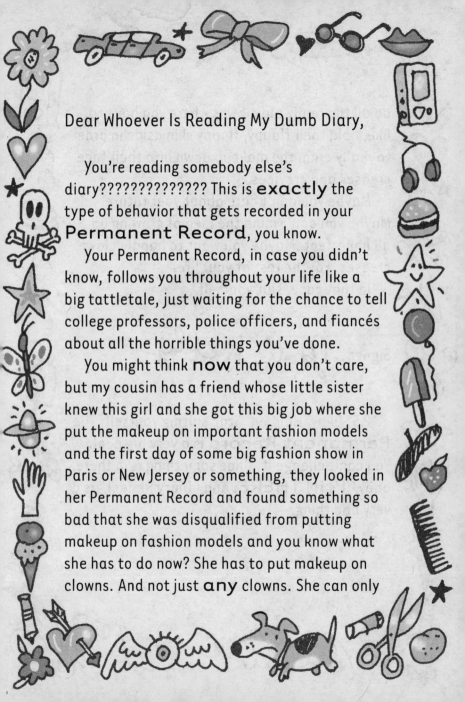

Dear Whoever Is Reading My Dumb Diary,

You're reading somebody else's diary??????????????? This is **exactly** the type of behavior that gets recorded in your **Permanent Record**, you know.

Your Permanent Record, in case you didn't know, follows you throughout your life like a big tattletale, just waiting for the chance to tell college professors, police officers, and fiancés about all the horrible things you've done.

You might think **now** that you don't care, but my cousin has a friend whose little sister knew this girl and she got this big job where she put the makeup on important fashion models and the first day of some big fashion show in Paris or New Jersey or something, they looked in her Permanent Record and found something so bad that she was disqualified from putting makeup on fashion models and you know what she has to do now? She has to put makeup on clowns. And not just **any** clowns. She can only do all the really old clowns where you have to, like, hold their flappy, floppy skin aside in order to really cram the makeup down into their face creases and crevices.

Maybe you don't care about your future. Maybe you don't mind the idea of growing up all imperfect. Maybe you want to handle clown creases. For the rest of your life.

In that case, suit yourself.

Signed, *Jamie Kelly*

P.S. Okay. Hold on. Stop suiting yourself. The **Permanent Record** is a very big deal. You can't change it. Once something is in there, baby, it's **IN THERE**, and "Diary Reader" is a very bad thing.

SUNDAY 01

Dear Dumb Diary,

You know the sound a coconut makes when it bounces off the rubbery side of a prize-winning hog?
Wait.
I'm getting ahead of myself.
Let me describe my Friday.
Let's say that you had a best friend and her name was, I don't know, Shmisabella. Okay, so Shmisabella is taking banjo lessons. She told you so and proved it by showing you her banjo case. She even played you some banjo music she has on her iPod — "I am way into banjos," Shmisabella says — but here's the thing: Shmisabella does **NOT**, in any way, have anything to do with the banjo. You just don't know that yet.

Perhaps you were at lunch a week before, and your friend said something about how one time she brought a kangaroo home from the zoo.

Sure, *you* know that Shmisabella actually did it, because it was your garage she hid the kangaroo in until she climbed into the kangaroo's pouch and you had to confess to your parents so they would call the paramedics to come and remove her from a kangaroo.

But another girl at the table, Yolanda, who is a dainty person — you know the type, eats popcorn one piece at a time, has those tiny little buttons on her clothing that people with regular human-sized hands can't operate — made this quiet, dainty *pfft* sound to indicate that she thought your friend was lying.

Now, Shmisabella didn't react to the *pfft* sound, so you knew that she either didn't care or just ignored it.

Yeah, guess what. **Wrong.** She noticed it.

The dainty also eat little sandwiches with tweezers.

2

You might think that your science teacher, Mrs. Curie, was out sick because teachers just normally get sick. Like maybe they got poisoned by that red ink they use to grade papers, or maybe the subject they teach finally just suffocated them in a big steaming pile of boredom.

You would never think that maybe Shmisabella had somehow **arranged** for the teacher to miss class that morning, maybe by calling her home and telling her that there was a large package waiting for her that had accidentally been delivered to a post office in the next town.

All of these things just don't add up until . . .

. . . until they all suddenly make sense when the substitute teacher bends over to pick up some papers that blew off the desk because *somebody* had piled them close to the edge and left a window open.

Then Shmisabella reaches forward, places the **tennis racquet** that she had been keeping in her banjo case into Yolanda's dainty hand, and throws a tennis ball at 100 miles per hour at the substitute's ample backside, making a sound a lot like a coconut bouncing off the rubbery side of a prize-winning hog. (You might recall I mentioned this earlier.)

Yolanda understood exactly how this looked, and since she's dainty, she's capable of swiftly slipping things like tennis racquets into another person's hand, **especially** if that person is kind of asleep and that person happens to be me.

s just like a ways: They bend rize-winning hogs when are good at figuring things out determining that the person holding the tennis racquet probably has something to do with the cooling ointment the substitute will be applying to their backside at lunch.

Now here's the surprise: This "Shmisabella" I've been telling you about is really Isabella, and all of this **really happened**. She tried to set up Yolanda for *pfft*ing her kangaroo story, and I, an attractive and innocent bystander, got caught up in the scandal.

The sub sent me down to the office to talk to the assistant principal, but he wasn't there, so I have to see him first thing tomorrow morning. I am SO SO SO SO SO SO SO SO SO SO SO SO telling on Isabella.

That is It, Isabella!

RAGE FUME ANGER

I'm turning you IN!

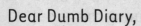

Dear Dumb Diary,

    I didn't tell on Isabella.

    I met with the assistant principal, who also happens to be my uncle now because he married my Aunt Carol. He also happens to be Angeline's uncle, through some sort of profoundly tragic bad luck that involves Angeline being related to him.

    He told me that he had read what the substitute said about the tennis ball incident, and wondered why I would ever choose a tennis ball as the projectile. He said that he remembered my Aunt Carol trying to teach me how to play tennis over the summer. During the course of an hour, he saw me hit the ball only three times, and all of those times were with my neck.

    But he said he knew that Yolanda, who sits next to me in science, is actually quite an excellent tennis player, and that a tennis ball is exactly what somebody would expect **her** to use.

GLUK

World Champion
of Ladies'
Neck Tennis

6

But Yolanda, being dainty, just isn't the type that gets into this kind of trouble. Uncle Dan suspected that maybe Isabella had something to do with this whole thing, because he checked and it turns out that she was in town when it occurred.

I asked him how he knew Yolanda was good at tennis, and he waved a folder at me.

"It's in her **Permanent Record**," he said. "Along with grades and behavior, we keep track of all your extracurricular activities."

And then he opened my folder to show me all of my extracurricular activities which, as it turns out, **didn't exist**.

He pointed out that I've never joined a school club or played on a school team or anything like that.

I explained to him that it was okay because those things were for weenies and I had never been, nor planned to ever be, any sort of weenie. I just don't see **weenieism** as an option in my future.

He said that colleges look at these sorts of things and it was time that I gave that some thought. One day, he said, I would have to grow up and work for a living, which I think we can all agree is a pretty **awful** way to punish a person just for the crime of growing up.

"Jamie," Uncle Dan said, "I want you to try some extracurriculars. You might like them. You might even make some new friends that aren't getting into trouble every couple of days."

"Like which friend of mine are you referring to? Angeline?" I asked, awesomely pretending not to know who he was really talking about.

He smiled. "I'm not going to punish Isabella or Yolanda. I don't have proof that they did anything wrong. I'm not going to punish you, because I know you can't play tennis and you have no sense of aim, even if the target was as wide as that substitute's . . ." He stopped himself and thought for a moment. **_Area of victimization._**

I nodded with enough innocence for both me and Isabella combined.

The NOD of INNOCENCE

The EYES OF VIRTUE

The TINY MOUTH OF THE RIGHTEOUS

The CLASPED HANDS of the BLAMELESS

And then, because there's probably a rule that no visit with an assistant principal can end perfectly well, he added, "Let's talk in a few weeks. I want you to try an extracurricular activity, and I want to hear your thoughts about your future. Your file is good, but there's no reason it can't be perfect."

Now I have to think about my future. *My future*. I liked my past better. I didn't have a future back then.

The ONLY things I worried about as a child

what if Mommy "PEEKS" but doesn't "A-BOO"?

What if Daddy Never gives my Nose BACK?

What if my Stinky diaper offends people?

Actually I couldn't care less.

TUESDAY 03

Dear Dumb Diary,

Before science class today, Mrs. Curie said that Assistant Principal Devon told her that I didn't have anything to do with the Tennis Balling of the Rump in Question, although I could tell by the way she kept her back to the wall during class that she wasn't convinced.

In between her quick turns, Mrs. Curie told us we're going on a **field trip** later this month to a science museum.

Field trips are awesome. I love them. I've thrown up twice on field trips, but nobody can detect throw-up on our buses. The kids are so loud and the buses already smell so terrible that you could barf up a deep-fried basketball shoe and nobody would notice.

It's **kind of nice** knowing you can throw up anytime you like. You don't often get that privilege in the real world.

PURE GROSSNESS

SCHOOL BUS

After class, I asked Isabella about her extracurriculars, since we are supposed to be doing stuff like that for college.

Isabella was surprised I was thinking about college.

"But you're *dumb*, Jamie," she said. "Not dumb like *Accidentally-Ate-the-Wrapper-on-the-Taco Dumb*. You're more like **Dumb-About-Stuff-That-You-Really-Shouldn't-Be-Dumb-About**."

"What does that even mean?" I demanded.

"It's hard to explain," Isabella said. "Maybe if you were smarter, it would be easier. Look at it this way: Angeline is the pretty one who is also nice and smart, I'm the smart one who is also pretty and nice, and you're the dumb one with pretty friends."

By this time, Angeline had walked up and overheard Isabella's conclusions.

Angeline laughed. "I don't think you have that totally correct," she said. "You're not *that* nice, Isabella."

Evidently, there are SEVERAL different kinds of DUMBNESS

AFRAID OF CLOUDS DUMB

BITES TOENAILS DUMB

TALKS TO CANDY DUMB

BLOND

"WAIT A SECOND," I said angrily and totally correctly.

I pointed out that my grades are really pretty good (better than Isabella's, anyway), and I know quite a few very large words, although I was a little spitty and sputtery when I was saying that so I couldn't remember any of them off the top of my head. But I couldn't help it. I was angry.

"How long have you thought I was the dumb one?" I demanded.

Isabella shrugged and said forever. Angeline said she thought we should talk about something else, like koala bears, which I know she was just doing to get me off the subject. It became so obvious to me after I suddenly realized that for the last ten minutes I had been talking about koala bears.

Just wait until they get a load of my future, which is going to be **perfect**.

EXPERTS AGREE

KOALAS CAN DISTRACT YOU FROM

ANYTHING.

SO YOU MUST NEVER OPERATE A KOALA while you are driving.

BE careful, people

WEDNESDAY 04

Dear Dumb Diary,

So today after school, I took a bold step toward the future by joining my first extracurricular activity, **the Chess Club.**

Chess is a very interesting game, and like so many interesting games, it is not in any way fun. It looks like four horses lost amongst a variety of pepper mills and salt shakers, and the objective is to remain awake longer than your opponent.

The Chess Club people insist that it is a blast, but if it was really so great, you have to wonder why people would have worked so hard for so long to invent more entertaining things, like watching television and **not playing chess.**

JUST A FEW THINGS THAT ARE MORE FUN THAN PLAYING CHESS

WAtching FRuit Spoil

Everything else in the WORLD

Just quietly sitting

Then I took another step toward my future (a chessless future, that is), and decided to **never attend** another Chess Club meeting.

I'm not worried. I'll discover the right extracurricular activity. Besides, I want a little extra time to spend on science. When we go to that science museum, I'm going make it very clear that I am **not** the dumb one.

Here are just a few perfectly scientific things I'll do:

science → pose

Correctly identify the museum from other nearby buildings like a gas station or Taco Bell.

Look carefully at the exhibits and remain mostly awake for most of the field trip.

Not make the mistake of trying to order a taco at the museum like last time.

THURSDAY 05

Dear Dumb Diary,

Today was Meat Loaf Day. I'm not sure if I've mentioned this to you before, but every Thursday is Meat Loaf Day at our school.

I know, I know. How bad can it be, right? I mean, it's made out of meat, and many of our favorite things are made out of meat: steaks, salami, my legs.

And it's formed into a loaf, and I love loaf-shaped objects. I love bread. I love Grandma.

But there's something about how my school prepares the meat loaf that makes it terrible. Maybe it's the type of beef they use, or the demons that cast evil spells on it, or the seasonings. I don't know.

It's probably the demons or the seasonings.

JUST BECAUSE SOMETHING IS MEAT LOAF-SHAPED DOESN'T MEAN IT'S BAD...

Like Grandma

OR money baked into A MEAT LOAF

Angeline eats the meat loaf every Thursday and doesn't complain **ever**, which proves, I think, that even if you are blessed with intense good looks, you can have the taste buds of one of those rats that lives at the dump and eats diapers.

One can only assume that these taste buds will grow and grow and grow until the taste buds take over and the person is entirely diaper-dump rat. Oh, did I say **assume**? I meant to say **hope**.

"Do you ever wonder why we eat this?" I asked, waggling a clump on the end of my plastic fork.

Isabella grinned.

"Well, if you're so smart, why don't you tell us?" she said, and a couple of people at our table laughed.

"Maybe I will," I said, wadding the lump up in a piece of napkin and sticking it in my backpack, because that's what scientists do: We take samples.

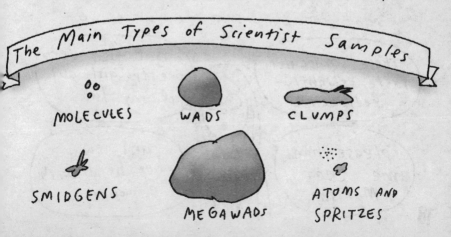

The Main Types of Scientist Samples

MOLECULES   WADS   CLUMPS

SMIDGENS   MEGAWADS   ATOMS AND SPRITZES

Angeline leaned in close enough for me to smell all nine of the distinct fragrances she was wearing.

"Jamie. Seriously. Don't worry about it. You're smart."

I shoved her away. Then I pulled her back for one more little sniff — because let's face it, she smells pretty good — and then shoved her away again.

"Angeline. The first rule of science is that The Smart Must Find Junk Out."

Okay, at the time I thought that sounded like something all the smart people would say, but now when I see it written, I'm not so sure. I should have said **SMARTNESS MARCHES ON** or **IMA GET ALL SMART UP IN HEYAH** or something like that.

Anyway.

MORE THINGS SAID BY THE SMART

These molecules taste slightly radioactive.

get that very pretty girl out of my lab.

please hand me that Martian.

and swap her head with a monkey's.

FRIDAY 06

Dear Dumb Diary,

So in science we're talking about animals now, which is pretty interesting because there are so many of them I like to **pet** and so many I like to **eat**. There are even a few that fall into both categories, which probably makes them really nervous about what I'm thinking when they see me coming.

We're learning about how animals adapt to their environments. Like, when ancient relatives of the elephant moved to colder environments, they evolved thick fur. When relatives of mine moved to colder environments, they evolved sweaters and complaining.

I felt like today was a good chance to begin my meat loaf analysis.

"Mrs. Curie," I said scientifically, "is there a reason for an animal to develop a bad taste so that nobody wants to eat it?"

Mrs. Curie looked a little surprised, like all teachers do when they realize you are **actually thinking**.

"Yes, Jamie. As a matter of fact, many animals taste bad, and it may be so that predators won't eat them."

"But what if it has no effect?" I continued, wishing I was wearing glasses so that I could remove them and touch the stem to my chin thoughtfully. "Some things taste bad, and people eat them anyway."

OMG
LooK How
I smart
I LooK

if I
had glasses
and did
this

Mrs. Curie peered around the room. I wondered if she was looking out for tennis balls before she turned around and wrote this on the board: **Why would people eat animals that taste bad?**

"Class," she said, "Jamie has an interesting question here, and it fits in with what we're studying."

People started calling out answers and she wrote them down.

1) STARVATION

2) NO OTHER CHOICE

3) IT'S GOOD FOR YOU

4) HATRED OF ANIMAL (ISABELLA SAID THIS ONE)

5) REVENGE AGAINST ANIMAL'S FAMILY (ALSO ISABELLA)

"It's none of those," I said. "None of those reasons apply here. I'm talking about the school meat loaf, and none of those reasons are the reason. We're not starving, we have other choices, it can't be that good for you, and except for Isabella, **nobody** hates cows."

"It's that nonstop cud chewing all the time," Isabella piped up. "Always with the cud. Have you ever tasted it? It's not that great. Plus, cows get all snorty when you take it from them."

Mrs. Curie paused for a moment while Isabella's comment sank in. Then she shook her head and moved on.

"Well, maybe it's because the meat loaf is so delicious, right?" she asked with a big hopeful grin. We all shook our heads **NO**.

I don't have my answer yet, so I'm going to have to do more science, but see? **I'M TELLING YOU, I'M NOT THE DUMB ONE.**

SHUT UP, COW. You'll get your CUD Back when I'm DONE With it.

After school today, I looked into another extracurricular activity. I'm surprised at how many there are at my school.

I haven't told Isabella about the conversation I had with Assistant Principal Uncle Dan yet, but there's a chance she already knows. Isabella likes to spy on me. There is a chance she is watching me right **NOW**.

I just whipped around to see if she was behind me and yelled **"NOW!"** as I wrote that.

She wasn't there, but Stinker was. He was a little startled and bit my ankle and choked on a Band-Aid that he pulled off my ankle and ate.

Maybe I shouldn't let him do that. But I don't know, it seems to make him happy to believe he's injured me by biting off some of my skin, and it doesn't bother me when he chokes a little. It's what you call a **win-win**. It's probably why we love each other so much.

so happy

23

I have to remember to let Stinker out of the closet before I go to sleep. (He's almost impossible to catch, but I tricked him into running in there by tossing in that meat loaf lump I still had in my backpack. It smells just enough like food to fool a fat old beagle.)

Back to today's extracurricular adventure.

I figured that my perfect future might want me to be a little more organized, so I went to this after-school thing called LET'S GET ORGANIZED, PEOPLE.

greed foam

meat clod

Nobody was there except the teacher supervisor, and she said that there actually are a lot more people signed up, but they keep forgetting to come, mostly because they aren't organized enough to write down when they're supposed to be there.

I figured that going to the meeting this one time already makes me one of the star members of the club, so I don't really need it anymore. Just like that, I decided to **never attend again**.

How to tell if You're Already Too Organized

1. If you always eat your food in alphabetical order.

2. If you keep your socks on hangers.

4. If you brush your hair one hair at a time.

3. If you always make sure your lists are in correct order.

Dear Dumb Diary,

Angeline and her mom drove past this morning and happened to catch me out in my front yard throwing small stones at a bush.

Look, I know that may seem like a waste of time, but it was just one of those things that you find yourself doing and you **can't explain why.** I also like to sit in the grass sometimes and tear out handfuls just to hear that pleasant ripping sound.

They stopped the car and Angeline hopped out. She was all dressed up in soccer stuff because she was headed to practice, and she asked if I wanted to go along. She said the coach would probably even let me play a bit to see if I liked it.

c'mon, Angeline. I'm kind of BUSY Here...

I **am** looking for some extracurricular things, and soccer **is** supposed to be a lot of fun, and it **is** really good exercise, and **lots** of people play. . . .

I said forget it.

But my mom was momfully standing in the doorway listening and mommishly told me to go. The only thing my mom likes making more than **making dinner** and **making beds** is **making me do stuff**.

Anyway, I put on some shorts and went along.

♥ Also, Mom L♥ves... ♥

SILLY WELCOME MATS

NEXT TIME BRING COOKIES

CAUSING CRIPPLING EMBARRASSMENT

JAMIE

Wonderful makeup you aren't allowed to touch and she doesn't use

I'm really not even sure why Angeline does extracurricular things. She's so beautiful that she's probably going to marry a billionaire one day or get some amazing job where they don't care if you get everything wrong all the time as long as you look good doing it.

That's right, I'm looking at *you*, Miss Weatherlady.

I learned that soccer is mostly about chasing a ball up and down a big field. I'm not sure how I feel about playing a sport that even a very fat beagle choking on a Band-Aid could easily beat me at.

Angeline makes it all seem very graceful, of course, effortlessly resembling an antelope — and at times, even a **unicorn antelope**, which everyone knows is the most graceful antelope ever born.

I looked a lot more like an orangutan hungrily chasing a melon while trying to free up a wedgie. After a very, very long and exhausting two full minutes of play, I decided that soccer is **not** the extracurricular for me.

GRUNT
WHEEZE
GRUNT
WHEEZE
GRUNT

PRANCE
SKIP
PRANCE

Angeline was a little disappointed, saying that she'd hoped I would join her team. I had to tell her that it wouldn't fit into my schedule very well because I had something else to do **every Saturday forever.**

I made sure that I sounded very not-dumb when I said it, too, because I'm still mad at her for thinking that I'm dumb.

I even remembered to let Stinker out of the closet just now. Would **THE DUMB ONE** have remembered that? Huh?

Okay, it's about a day late, but I remembered.

PROOF I'M NOT DUMB

could probably easily invent a chemical or robot or whatever

Have always known that there's nobody REALLY THERE during those KNOCK-KNOCK jokes

Am skilled at NO LESS than SIXTEEN extremely intelligent-looking poses

Dear Dumb Diary,

Isabella came over to work on homework today. She and I agree that homework strongly indicates that the teachers are not doing their jobs well enough during the school day. It's not like they'll let you bring your **home stuff** to school and work on it there. You can't say, "I didn't finish sleeping at home, so I have to work on finishing my sleep here."

Before we started on the homework, I told her about my little soccer outing with Angeline, and she asked why I went along with it.

"Well, my mom was —" I began, and Isabella put a finger over my lips and nodded. Any explanation that begins, "*Well, my mom . . .*" really doesn't need to be finished.

My little talk with Uncle Dan is still bugging me. I asked Isabella if she ever worried about her future, like going to college and getting a job and all that stuff.

She laughed so hard in my face that I not only knew she'd had bacon for breakfast, I could tell you **how many pieces**.

"Jamie!" she scoffed. "You really *are* dumb, aren't you? It's pretty obvious what I'm going to do for a living one day, isn't it?"

There was **no way** I was going to be the dumb one.

"Yes. Oh, yeah. Of course. I mean, sure. It's obvious. I mean, yes. Yes, I know. I always knew. One time I thought I didn't know and then I realized that I totally knew. Yes. Yes. Yes. Yes, I know," I said convincingly.

"Yes," I added to make it extra extra-convincing.

And then I added a kind of loud "Yup," so that there was no doubt that I knew.

I have no idea.

P.S. It was three pieces of bacon.

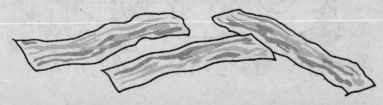

Dear Dumb Diary,

Here's how math class went down today.

Listen, when you are a beautiful young girl who needs people to understand that you are not an imbecile, math may not be doing you any favors.

I've really picked my grades up in math, and I've learned that math is pretty much just a big bully. Like any bully, he'll try his best to scare and intimidate you, but if you stand up to him and show him you're not scared, there is a very good chance that he'll make things **even worse**.

Anyway, I've also discovered that I can do math, although it requires some concentration and focus and memorization and something else that I don't remember.

Today Mr. Henzy asked me to go up to the board and complete a problem. You know, I'm fine when it's just me and my paper and pencil working on the numbers. I'm just never ready to do it in front of people. I can do it, but there's going to be a transformation occurring that I am not anxious to let others witness. I can do the problem, but There Will Be Scowling. There Will Be Wrinkles. There Will Be Fingernail Chewage.

Why do we have to do things in front of people to prove that we can? I brush my teeth by myself, and nobody has ever asked me to prove I can do that.

I brush my teeth every morning to see what I'll look like if I go crazy that day

I didn't want to go to the board, and what I thought was an excellent question suddenly occurred to me, so I shared it with Mr. Henzy.

"Mr. Henzy," I asked, "didn't somebody complete this exact same problem in your class last year?"

"Yes," he said.

"And probably every year, for many years before that?"

"Yes, I suppose."

I had him right where I wanted him.

"Don't you think it's time that you finally **accepted** the answer? The rest of us have all accepted it, Mr. Henzy, and we feel like it's time to move on."

OMG I would be SUCH a great TALK SHOW HOST

About one second later, in the assistant principal's office, my Uncle Dan looked at me across his big desk. He was looking very principally and not very **unclish**.

Or **uncley**. Would the word be **uncley**? Anyway.

"Jamie, you usually don't have this many run-ins with teachers. First with Mrs. Curie, and now with Mr. Henzy," he said sternly.

"He started it," I said, knowing that wouldn't work as the words left my mouth. It's really too bad that you can't catch things when they're between your mouth and the other person's ears. So I added:

"Math is a huge pain in the . . . Area of Victimization."

UNCLEY   PRINCIPALLY   PANDISH

(I've never actually seen this one, I'm just sayin')

Uncle Dan smiled.

"Well, I must say that I am very pleased that you took my advice," he said, thumping my file with his hand. "I see here in your Permanent Record that you've signed up for several extracurriculars, and even started playing soccer."

Well, I **DID** sign up for the extracurriculars. I decided to never go to them ever, ever, ever again, but what he said is technically true, and let's face it, technically true is a lot like true true.

And I **DID** start playing soccer. The fact that I stopped two minutes later didn't really have to come up.

And then I understood.

It's a **PERMANENT** Record. Permanent. Like, it can't be erased. They know that you signed up, but they don't know that you quit, and you get to go to college anyway. This may explain why so many lazy people graduate.

Lazy surgeon who makes people do their own stitches

I didn't see Isabella for the rest of day, so I had to wait to call her until after one of Mom's **homemade dinners**.

That might sound good, but just because things are homemade, it doesn't mean they're good.

House fires, for example, are homemade.

Even Stinker wouldn't take anything I slipped him under the table, and I once saw Stinker eat two square feet of tablecloth.

(He could have eaten more tablecloth, but some of Mom's casserole had spilled on it and so he stopped.)

More Homemade Goodness

THAT NOBODY LIKES

Frankenstein

Bathroom after Dad uses it.

Bathroom after Frankenstein uses it. (NOT AS BAD)

When we finally talked on the phone, Isabella was surprised and pleased by my discovery.

"So the Permanent Record has a **flaw**, does it?" she asked, with the same kind of joy that a troll expresses when he asks if you meant it when you said he could eat your kitten. "I always knew there had to be something wrong with it, and you found that something, Jamie."

I imagined her finishing off the rest of the kitten.

"Well, yes, I guess I did," I said, blushing modestly. "I'm blushing modestly," I added, because she couldn't see me over the phone.

"This flaw, I don't think it's good for anything, but I **take back** what I said before," Isabella said. "I take back what I said about you being the dumbest person I know."

"Thanks, Isab —"

"And lazy. And messy. And clumsy. All of it. I take it all back," she went on.

"Thanks, Isab —"

"You're still dumb. Just not **THE** dumbest."

Pretty cool, huh? **NOT THE DUMBEST.** That's going to look pretty good on my business card one day.

congratulations, Miss kelly. You're HIRED! You weren't the DUMBEST one that applied for the job.

TUESDAY 10

Dear Dumb Diary,

Mrs. Curie stopped me today as I was walking into science class.

"**The meat loaf,**" she said.

"The meat loaf," I responded.

"What's the deal with the meat loaf?" she asked.

"That's what I always say," I said, because I always say that.

She told me that she had been thinking more about it. She thought that I had asked some pretty good questions.

"And now that you have your answers, I guess we can be done with it, **hmmm?**" she said, nodding slightly.

SCIENCE IS SCUPER!

known Isabella almost my whole life, and Isabella has tried to convince me to do something I shouldn't do almost every single day of that life. If there is **ONE THING** I know for sure, it's when somebody is trying to lead me to a conclusion.

All I could think was, *Seriously, Mrs. Curie, I've been manipulated by the best. Spare me.*

"Yeah," I said, knowing that it was what I was supposed to say. I narrowed my eyes at her. She narrowed hers back.

Not wanting to be outnarrowed, I narrowed my eyes more, and she responded with even narrower eyes. We continued narrowing until I realized that my eyes were **closed** and I couldn't walk to my desk that way.

Isabella was waiting for me by my locker the end of the day, and said that we were joining an after-school extracurricular. She quickly grabbed Angeline's backpack from the floor as we ran so that Angeline would have to follow us.

When we got to where we were going, there were about ten boys in the classroom. **No girls.** They all stared blankly at us as we walked in.

"We're joining this extracurricular," Isabella said to the teacher that was supervising. (He was one of those teachers that you see all the time but never know their name. He is kind of average-looking and dresses pretty average. He has sort of an average personality and is of an average height and weight. I just call him Mr. Ugly.)

"Not so fast," one of the boys objected. "You have to really be a gamer to join this club. What games do you ladies play?" There was something very **insulting** and **challenging** about the way he lisped the question at us. All of the other dorks stared at us, waiting for an answer.

Then Angeline walked in, looking for her backpack.

You never get used to the sound of NERD GROWLS

This caused all the gamers to sort of avert their eyes from Angeline, as if they weren't worthy to gaze upon her.

They were right about that, of course — **they aren't**. But I think that they also should not have been quite so comfortable gazing upon me, either.

"Give me my backpack," Angeline said, pausing for a moment and then mumbling, "It smells like pizza in here, and a little bit like somebody is wearing . . ."

"Wearing what?" I asked.

She leaned in and whispered to me, "You've heard of antiperspirants. Is there such a thing as a *pro-perspirant*?"

"You'll get your backpack after we join this club," Isabella interrupted. "Doofus McDerpydiaper here won't let us sign up."

"Why don't **you** ask him?" I suggested to Angeline, and she smiled at the lisper.

I remember some goofy giggling, and faces blushing so red you couldn't even see the acne anymore. The next thing you know, Angeline was elected president of the Videogamer Club for life, and Isabella and I became her vice presidents.

It turns out that we were the first three girls to ever try to join, and the fact that we're never going to attend again probably won't bother them at all.

Gamers have a great sense of adventure and a great love of legend, and I imagine **The Tale of the Three Gorgeous Gamers** will be told and retold in front of flickering screens over sloshing glasses of Mountain Dew and snacks covered in that bright orange cheese-flavored sand.

And now I have **ANOTHER** extracurricular activity on my record.

After Angeline had twinkled away with her backpack, I asked Isabella why she wanted to participate in extracurriculars all of a sudden.

"Last night, my dad and my older brothers got into this huge argument. He said they were lazy good-for-nothings and would probably end up living at home, lying around, doing nothing for the rest of their lives," Isabella said.

"That's pretty upsetting," I said.

"I'll say," Isabella agreed. "Lying around, doing nothing for the rest of my life in my parents' house was MY plan. But I don't want to live there if my brothers are going to be there, too. I guess now I have to get into college, Jamie, and that means I need my extracurriculars, too."

Lying around doing nothing is way less appealing when it's forever.

WEDNESDAY 11

Dear Dumb Diary,

In Language Arts today, Mrs. Avon (English teacher and possessor of gums big enough for several much larger English teachers) is having us write news articles about something happening at school.

She wants us to be able to communicate big ideas quickly in a way that will make people want to read more.

Incredibly, Isabella finished the assignment weeks early. Here it is:

FLIRTY ART TEACHER, MISS ANDERSON, SHOWS UP AT SCHOOL WEARING DEODORANT.

WE BELIEVE THAT, IN FACT, SHE WEARS DEODORANT TO SCHOOL ALL OF THE TIME, JUST LIKE THE REST OF THE TEACHERS.

Mrs. Avon and Isabella got into a little discussion about the assignment, and Mrs. Avon said Isabella's headline was inappropriate. Isabella asked her if she had any reason to believe that anything in it was untrue.

"Some of the teachers **NOT** wearing deodorant?" she asked Mrs. Avon. "Perhaps you would like to make a statement on the record?"

I think it was because Isabella had her little pen and paper poised to take notes on Mrs. Avon's response that the discussion came to an end.

"Fine. How does a B minus grab you?" Mrs. Avon asked her.

"Make it a B, and we're good," Isabella said. And with that, Isabella was done **weeks** ahead of schedule.

She's good.

Maybe Isabella is going to grow up to be somebody that negotiates big deals, or a rhinoceros trainer.

If they ever clone these things, she'd be good at training them.

Because Isabella is already done with her assignment and Mrs. Avon knows that this sort of project is a breeze for me, she said okay when Isabella asked if we could be excused from class to work on a project for **the Student Awareness Committee**, which, I was told in an aggressive whisper moments before, was an extracurricular club we had very recently joined.

Actually, we didn't just join it.

Isabella informed me out in the hall that we had just **created** it.

"It occurred to me, Jamie, why should we just join clubs when we can invent as many as we want? That's **got** to look good on our Permanent Records."

It's pretty hard to argue with Isabella's logic. Mostly because when you do, she's pretty hard on you.

And I think she's right. I can already feel my future becoming **perfecter**.

Sometimes when Isabella wants to make a point

she does it with something pointy

THURSDAY 12

Dear Dumb Diary,

You know, it wasn't that long ago that I saw Angeline as an enemy — the kind of enemy that never really does anything bad or is mean or has anything wrong with them in any way. You know the kind of enemy I mean: **The Worst Kind**.

It used to bother me that the boys, and in particular, Hudson Rivers (eighth-cutest boy in my grade), were all infatuated with her beautiful looks and wonderful personality and niceness and all of that horrible, horrible, horrible garbage.

But I'm more mature now, and I've accepted Angeline as a **FRIEND UNTIL FURTHER NOTICE**. Plus, I am able to believe that the boys are all infatuated with her because she's friends with me and I find that comforting.

Shut up, Diary. This works for me.

Let's face it...

I'm Angeline's best quality.

And since Angeline is a friend (until further notice), she sits with us at lunch quite often.

"You want to sign up for the Student Awareness Committee?" Isabella asked her.

"Never heard of it," Angeline said, slowly sawing at her meat loaf.

"It's a new club here," Isabella explained.

"Can't be," Angeline said. "I'd know about it."

"It is," Isabella said, somewhat angrily. "I happen to **know** it is, Miss Stupidpants, because *I* started it."

"Stupidpants, huh?" Angeline said, after she politely squeezed down a bite of meat loaf.

I don't think "Miss Stupidpants" is even a thing. Sometimes Isabella comes up with insults off the top of her head.

"PENGUIN FART"   "Prince Dinglestink"   "Cow Lady"

Isabella rubbed her chin as if she had a beard. This was not hard to picture, as her grandma really does have a little beard, and you can see the family resemblance.

The MAIN Beards I'd choose for Isabella

chicken seller

president

comes WITH FREE WART

weirdo guy

tiny musician style

I've learned that Angeline, though beautiful, knows a lot more than you'd sometimes think, and **"Miss Stupidpants"** was probably over the line.

"That's right. **Miss Stupidpants,**" Isabella repeated, choosing to stay on that side of the line.

Just then, Bruntford, a storm cloud that can often pass for a lunchroom monitor, shambled past, eyeing our trays as she went.

Normally we avert our gaze, not wanting to be **turned to stone** and all, but I suddenly remembered my science and stopped her.

"Miss Bruntford, can I ask you a question about the meat loaf for my science class? Nobody likes it. Why does the cafeteria sell it?"

I once saw this documentary about some wolves that had cornered a bison, and it had exactly the same look on its face as Bruntford. You know, if bison were uglier and smaller.

"Who is your science teacher again?" she asked, trying to smile.

"Mrs. Curie," I said. "But why does that matter? Why does the cafeteria serve this?"

BRUNTFORD

HALF BISON, HALF STORM CLOUD, HALF ANOTHER BISON WHICH IS EVEN MEANER THAN THE FIRST HALF BISON

Bruntford walked away without answering. "Why wouldn't she answer?" Hudson asked handsomely. "It's a simple question."

FAMOUS UNANSWERED
-QUESTIONS-

FRIDAY 13

Dear Dumb Diary,

    Isabella and her mom picked me up early for school today. As it turns out, there are two extracurricular clubs that meet in the morning, and this morning, Isabella made me join them both.

    I am really beginning to wonder if including Isabella on this whole thing was such a good idea. It's important for me to have a perfect future, of course, but if Isabella's is perfecter than mine, I'm going to be spending some of my future trying to **sabotage** hers. Look, I know that's not a very attractive thing to say, but Isabella and I are very close friends and that's just what very close friends do.

    Our first stop was the Agriculture Club, which I suppose meets first thing in the morning because farmers get up really early.

But why? Isn't the farmer the **BOSS** of the farm? What's going to happen, are the cows going to just spray their milk all over the floor and make him mop it up if he's not there on time?

Seriously, farmers, take control. And cows, knock it off. I'll send Isabella over there, and you **know** how she feels about cows.

We were there just long enough to sign up and then leave, but nobody noticed because they were all too sleepy from being farmers.

The next stop was the Running Club. Everybody that participates in Track Team at school is in this club. It also attracts kids that do other sports, and people that enjoy waking up very early and running for the fun of it.

The. Fun. Of. It.

You know, how like when you see reports on TV of people running from volcanoes or escaped bears or things like that and they're all laughing and giggling about how much fun they're having and how they hope they get to just keep running and running and never stop.

We signed up and started walking away, since this is how we do things, but Yolanda stopped us. She had dragged over the teacher who supervises the Running Club, Mr. Dover.

"Jamie and Isabella just signed up. Can they run with us this morning?" she asked him daintily.

"Oh, no thanks," I said, and then I said **"Errff"** because that's what you say when Isabella punches you in the back.

"Yeah. We'd like that," Isabella said.

Mr. Dover said it was okay, and Isabella and I started running along, trying to keep up with the big group of Early Morning Runners who are more commonly known to normal people as **lunatics**.

THAT'S RIGHT. There are actually people that RUN when they could NOT RUN INSTEAD.

Wheeeeeeee

Run

"Why . . . did . . . you . . . say . . . we . . . would . . . run?" I asked Isabella as I gulped for oxygen.

"We don't want anybody discovering what we're doing. **Nobody** can find out about this flaw in the Permanent Record," she said without gasping. Isabella often has to wrestle both of her mean older brothers at once, and this has given her excellent breath control.

We watched as the more experienced runners pulled away from us.

"One . . . more . . . thing," I said, huffing. "Did . . . you . . . bring . . . any . . . clothes . . . to . . . change . . . into?"

WHEEZE
GRUNT
WHEEZE

She hadn't. And we were trailing so far beyond the other runners that we didn't even have time to duck into the locker room and shower when we finally finished.

As we were hurrying to get to class on time, although it's hard to hurry when you're all jiggly-legged, I realized that we were a little smelly from running. Not very smelly, of course, but experience has taught me that by lunchtime it was going to be worse. **Much worse.** Think: bologna sandwich left out on the counter all morning.

I had no perfume, no cologne, and no deodorant — nothing. And then a fragrance hit us right between the nostrils as we passed the Teachers' Lounge.

It smelled kind of flowery, and definitely sophisticated. It was a mature scent, and yet somehow playful and innocent.

"Here," Isabella said. "In here." She opened the door and pulled me through with her.

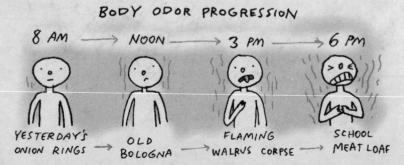

BODY ODOR PROGRESSION

8 AM ⟶ NOON ⟶ 3 PM ⟶ 6 PM

YESTERDAY'S ONION RINGS ⟶ OLD BOLOGNA ⟶ FLAMING WALRUS CORPSE ⟶ SCHOOL MEAT LOAF

We were in **the Teachers' Lounge**.

We had heard stories of this place, of course — the wild parties, the strange rituals, the plump comfy cushions stuffed with confiscated notes.

But there was no evidence of any of that. If anything, it was pretty boring and simple. The colors were on the drab side, the cushions not plump at all.

The teachers had probably just left for class. A coffeepot simmered on the burner. This alone stood out from the shabby surroundings, because the aroma was heavenly.

"I don't even like coffee, but I've never smelled anything so good," I said.

Isabella had already found the bag of grounds and was examining it carefully.

"This is expensive coffee," she said. **"Really expensive."**

We looked around. There was a half-eaten box of bargain donuts on the table. The refrigerator was full of normal-looking lunches in Tupperware containers. The flowers in the vase on the table were plastic. Nothing in the lounge was expensive — except the coffee.

Isabella dug her hand into the bag, reached under her shirt, and rubbed a handful of coffee grounds into her armpit.

I ran toward the door. I knew what was coming next. But Isabella stopped me.

"You said it yourself," she whispered. "This smells great. We don't have a choice. You want to smell like my Uncle Ned all day? It's better than nothing."

One time, I had dinner at Isabella's house and she and I had to sit next to her Uncle Ned. Uncle Ned smells like every smell every person can smell like, **ALL AT ONCE**. They used to sit him next to an open window, but the neighbors started to complain. **The neighbors in Canada.**

I cautiously inhaled the coffee scent from the bag. It smelled so good that, the next thing you know, I was also applying the grounds to myself.

We dusted our hands off, peeked carefully out the door, and then ran to class.

Teachers like me. I said, they **LIKE** me. They don't love me. But today, it was different.

They smiled at me more. They joked with me more. Even Mrs. Curie, who has been on edge with me about this whole meat loaf business, didn't get upset when I asked if she thought that wild dogs would have bailed on evolution if they had known they were going to end up as **French Poodles**.

The reason why the teachers were all so cheery didn't occur to me until lunch, when Angeline sat down between me and Isabella.

"Do you smell that?" Angeline asked us, taking a big inhale of the air around us.

"The coffee?" I asked. "Nope," I said quickly, realizing that wasn't the right way to answer her question.

"Did you two bring coffee for lunch?" she said, studying our lunches.

"No," Isabella said. "Stop smelling us. Stop smelling everything."

Bruntford rumbled past. From behind, we saw her huge frame stop and turn around. She was smiling.

"How are you ladies today?" she asked pleasantly.

Two things you never want to see rise: The Dead, and Isabella's eyebrow.

Isabella's eyebrow rose.

"Hey, Bruntford," Isabella said, making a point to call her only by her last name. "We were thinking of having candy for lunch on Monday. You cool with that?"

Actually, none of Isabella's eyebrow movements are terribly comforting.

Bruntford takes her lunchroom monitoring very seriously, and eating candy for lunch is the type of thing that could make a great angry flume of water spray out of her blowhole.

"Well, okay. Just this once. Have a nice day, ladies," she said and waddled away.

Isabella looked at me and grinned.

"It's the coffee," she said quietly, motioning toward her armpit. "They like how we smell."

At first I didn't believe it. But smells **do** have a powerful effect on people, and teachers **do** love their coffee.

TEACHER — COFFEE

DOG — MEAT

CHILD — CUPCAKE

DAD — COFFEE, MEAT, CUPCAKE, WHATEVS

SATURDAY 14

Dear Dumb Diary,

Isabella pounded on our front door at 8:30 this morning. **ON A SATURDAY.** You know who's up at 8:30 on a Saturday? Nobody. At 8:30, you can look outside and see birds and squirrels just lying on the sidewalks, fast asleep.

"Jamie!" she said in a rigid, over-rehearsed tone, "I have forgotten my school assignment in my locker at school and must go there to acquire it."

"Acquire?" I asked. "*Acquire*?"

"It's Saturday," my mom said hoarsely, still struggling with some morning voice. "What makes you think you can even get into the school?"

"There are clubs and sports and so forth," Isabella recited stiffly. "They use the school on Saturdays. An example of one is the Drama Club, who are preparing for the school play, which is called *Oklahoma!* But my parents aren't home right now, and I don't think the school is open for long."

I didn't know what she was up to, but I knew it wasn't homework. And I knew that Isabella was going to blow it.

Even this early in the morning, she was a little too rehearsed for my mom. I had to save it.

"**Forget it**, Isabella," I said. "You'll just have to miss the assignment. Who cares if you don't do some homework?"

MEDDLE!

WHOOSH

SUDDENLY— SUPER MOM WOMAN HEARS SOMEBODY SUGGEST THAT SOME HOMEWORK GETS BLOWN OFF—

"Oh, no you won't," Mom said, snapping at the bait like a big drowsy trout. "I'll drive you up there myself. Jamie, go get ready."

Works every time.

Isabella came up to my room with me while I got dressed. I told her that I couldn't believe she wasn't better at lying. Usually her lies are like a type of ballet.

"Whatever. Let's get on with your plan," she said.

"MY plan? It's YOUR PLAN," I objected.

She said that as soon as I stepped in and helped sell the story to my mom, I had taken partial ownership of the plan. That clumsy lying was all an act, I see now, to get me in on this.

She bounced happily out of my room, swinging her backpack over her shoulder.

"Let's go," she said.

When we got to the school, my mom waited in the car. The front door was unlocked, so we walked quickly through the empty halls. I stopped by Isabella's locker. She kept walking.

"Isn't your homework in here?" I called after her.

She kept walking . . . right up to the Teachers' Lounge. She knocked on the door and listened.

No answer.

"Isabella!" I whispered. **"What are you doing?"**

"Just keep watch."

She was in and out in a blink — and she had a sandwich bag half-filled with the special coffee.

She tucked the coffee into her backpack, pulled out a small bottle of perfume, and squirted us both a few times.

"So your mom won't smell the coffee," she said. Then she pulled a homework assignment out of her backpack to wave at my mom as we trotted back out to the car.

Isabella had tricked me into being a coffee-stealing accomplice, and had tricked my mom into driving the getaway car.

SUNDAY 15

Dear Dumb Diary,

Isabella and I spent the morning **whisperyelling** at each other on the phone.

"What if we had been caught? What would we tell my mom?"

"What if we were elephants? What if the moon explodes? What if spelling matters? These are all ridiculous questions. We *weren't* caught, Jamie. And now we have the coffee," she said.

"What are you thinking of doing with that, anyway?"

"I haven't figured it out yet. But this is powerful voodoo, Jamie. You saw how it worked."

And then she told me we have another extracurricular to sign up for tomorrow.

I questioned, in very intelligent terms, if we should even be continuing with the plan to fill our Permanent Records with extracurriculars, since it was leading us down a very dark path. "A path as dark as the darkest espresso," I said solemnly.

But then Isabella complimented me on the espresso metaphor, and I kind of forgot that I was concerned.

What is Isabella Going To Be??

Master Jewel Thief?

Woman who captures Master Jewel thieves?

Inhuman EATER OF SOULS OR DENTAL HYGIENIST?

MONDAY 16

Dear Dumb Diary,

Angeline walked slowly past my locker today and took a deep breath. I know she was smelling me, because I may have done the exact same move to her on several occasions.

"How weird are you, smelling people?" I asked, all disgusted.

"No coffee today, huh?" Angeline said knowingly.

"No," I said.

"Too bad. You know who's **crazy** about coffee? Hudson. I know that you're kind of over him and everything, but he loves the stuff."

"You're right, Angeline. I am over him," I said, with the careless sort of shrug that only the **TRULY OVER** can shrug.

The Normal Shrug

The TOTALLY OVER IT shrug

A few minutes later, I pushed Isabella up against a stall in the girls' bathroom and started digging into her backpack.

"I need some of that coffee," I said. Isabella opened the bag, and I scooped some out and began rubbing it on my neck and wrists like a fancy perfume. As I checked my hair in the mirror, I realized that Yolanda had stepped out of a stall and was watching us.

"What is that? Dirt?" she asked. "Brownie mix?"

Isabella moved toward her. Yolanda swallowed hard. All the dainty in the world couldn't protect her from Isabella.

"Look, Isabella," she said nervously. "I'm sorry I made you guys run with us the other day. I was just trying to get back at you for the tennis ball thing."

I stopped Isabella before she could say anything.

"If she hadn't done that, we wouldn't have ever found out about this stuff," I reminded her quietly.

Daintyness won't protect you from Disease, Isabella, or Earthquakes.

Isabella thought for a minute.

"Yeah, okay, Yolanda. But not a word," Isabella warned, and I motioned to Yolanda to make a quick exit before Isabella changed her mind.

I suddenly smelled like a very pretty, very feminine Starbucks, so the lunch ladies were extra pleasant and Bruntford tried smiling at me again, which you would find kind of pleasant but mostly disturbing even if you were a bison.

Hudson was sitting with Angeline and Isabella when I got to our lunch table. I sat down right next to him, leaning in to give him a large inhale of my fragrance.

He looked at me, **repulsed**.

"What is that smell? Were you drinking coffee?" he groaned.

"I, uh, no, I just, I." Not my best explanation, I'll admit, but that's pretty much how I answered.

He got up and ran from the table.

"**He hates coffee,**" Angeline said. "Can't even stand the smell of it."

Nausea is not always what a young lady is going for

"You said he loved it!"

"*Now* do you want to tell me what's going on?" Angeline asked.

I looked over at Isabella, and she was trying not to laugh. "Everybody knows Hudson hates coffee," she said.

Angeline pursed her lips. "Jamie. You and I are friends. Why would you keep something from me?"

I was mad.

"Angeline, the next time you smell somebody and it occurs to you to tell them that somebody likes the smell of something, you shouldn't lie about it."

"I'll stop if you will," she said.

"Angeline, I've lied about smells, like — how many times, Isabella?"

"Maybe four times," Isabella said. "Probably only one time."

"Yeah, **ONE TIME**!" I yelled.

Seriously. After all I've done for Angeline, this is how she acts?

SERIOUSLY, ANGELINE...

what was going through your hair??

TUESDAY 17

Dear Dumb Diary,

Right after Mrs. Curie took attendance in science today, I raised my hand.

"Mrs. Curie, I have **another idea** about the meat loaf."

Mrs. Curie said it would have to wait until a different time. But then, without even raising her hand, Angeline said that she wanted to hear it. She's probably just trying to apologize to me for stinking out Hudson.

And then Hudson agreed, and then there was murmuring and head nodding and Mrs. Curie said, "Fine. Let's hear it."

"Well, I was thinking about the cow it came from. And how the farmer was probably always telling the cow to finish eating his cow food or whatever. And the farmer probably made the cow do special cow exercises and take special cow medicine."

Mrs. Curie stood there with her hands on her hips. "Right, the farmer wants to keep the cow big and healthy."

"No," I said. "If the farmer could sell the cow skinny and sick, he would be totally cool with that. It's all done for the benefit of the farmer, not the cow."

"And how does this relate to the meat loaf?" she asked.

"Maybe the meat loaf . . . maybe it's not for **our** benefit, either," I said. "Maybe we're like the cow."

I sat across from my Uncle Dan again. This time he looked a little more uncley than assistant principally.

"Again with Mrs. Curie?" he asked.

I told him about the conversation we were having and how Mrs. Curie was all wrong about me being *disruptive*. We were just talking.

"Mike Pinsetti was the one that started mooing," I said.

"Mike does that all the time," he said. "He's not mooing. I think that he breathes through his mouth."

Uncle Dan looked though my folder and smiled. I think he was on my side on this one.

"Wow," he said. "You're really in a lot of clubs now, I see. Lots of extracurriculars here!"

I nodded and looked away, afraid that I might **confess out my eyes.**

"You want me to talk to Mrs. Curie?" he offered.

I did want him to, but since I had recently been involved in a coffee robbery here at the school, I didn't think I deserved his help.

"No," I said. "Can I just wait here for a few minutes and pretend like you yelled at me?"

After sitting there for a few minutes, I asked him, "By the way, Uncle Dan, do YOU eat the meat loaf in the cafeteria? You should try it. It's really unspeakably awful."

Okay, maybe "UNSPEAKABLY AWFUL" wouldn't work on a menu. Here are a few other ways to describe the meat loaf to get people to try it.

"Adventure Loaf"

"Double-Dare-You Loaf"

"Vulture's Favorite"

"Not Pure Poison Loaf"

WEDNESDAY 18

Dear Dumb Diary,

    I had to work on my news story for Mrs. Avon in class today, and I didn't have any good ideas. I didn't mean to show any of my headline ideas to Mrs. Avon, but she read them over my shoulder.

STUDENT WRITES HEADLINE.
ALSO THAT LITTLE SENTENCE UNDER THE HEADLINE.

NOTHING HAPPENS ANYWHERE.
JOURNALISTS TAKE THE DAY OFF.

MEAT LOAF. NOBODY LIKES IT.
WHY IS IT SERVED?

BLONDS EVOLVED FROM SPIDERS.
"NOT SURPRISED," SAY ALL SCIENTISTS EVERYWHERE.

SHOULDERS, PEOPLE.

They were invented to keep you from reading private things.

She said she really liked it, and I told her that
I had made it up. Science isn't certain that blonds
evolved from spiders. It could have been scorpions
or ticks.

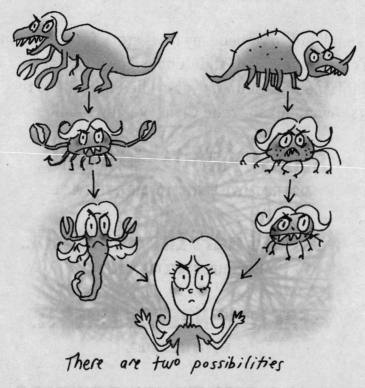

There are two possibilities

Turns out that it was the *meat loaf story*
that she liked.

"It asks a very simple but interesting
question, Jamie. I think I would read that article. Go
with it," she said with a big grin, and I leaned back a
bit to avoid being overexposed to gums.

After school, Isabella met me at my locker and we went to sign up for the Camera Club.

When we got there, everybody was showing each other their pictures on their computers, but since it's the Camera Club, you can **guess** what happens when new people walk in.

You would think that they would have torn up our applications right then and there, but they said Isabella will give them awesome practice if they decide to become paparazzi and they have to deal with **mentally disturbed celebrities**.

Isabella offered to hang around and punch a few more of them, but we had to make our next stop, the Cuisine Club.

The Cuisine Club was just the Cooking Club last year, but they changed the name to sound better. Sort of like how the **Student Fitness Club** used to be called **Gosh We're Fat**.

The Cuisine Club gets to use the cafeteria kitchen and, to tell you the truth, I think I might have actually **liked** being in this club except for how we're not actually being in any of the clubs we join.

My very beautiful art teacher, Miss Anderson, is the supervisor for this one. That makes a lot of sense, because a big part of food is the presentation, and that's why the most delicious foods in the world are so nice to look at.

Except maybe pizza, which looks like a manhole cover with a massive, unhealing wound.

Or spaghetti, which looks like a plateful of worms that were thrown through a fan.

Or chocolate —

You know, let's just **change the subject**.

The most beautiful way to present stew is hidden behind a food that **doesn't** so closely resemble chewed-up DOG FOOD.

When we got there, Miss Anderson was telling the group about how you have to budget a menu carefully. You need to think about what things cost. If you spend all your money on one thing, you won't have enough money for anything else.

I felt bad signing up and then leaving. We told Miss Anderson, like we tell all the rest of the club supervisors, that we'd be back next week, but we **won't**. We're just doing this to make our Permanent Records look better.

It's probably just like when a momma sea turtle buries her eggs in the sand. "I'll be right back," she says. "What? No, I wouldn't leave my babies all alone to crawl out into the ocean and try to learn to swim. That would be so super-lame."

I really wanted to confess to Miss Anderson. I wanted to admit what we were doing, but Isabella has us in too deep now.

Too deep.

I can honestly say that I've never felt turtlier.

me at my turtliest

THURSDAY 19

Dear Dumb Diary,

Hudson looked at me hesitantly at lunch.

"I didn't have any coffee. I don't smell," I reassured him.

He sat down across from me.

"I didn't know it bothered you so much," I said. "I thought **everybody** liked the smell of coffee."

He shrugged. "Not everybody. I know the teachers are all crazy about it. But I can't stand it."

Isabella and Angeline carried their trays over and sat down with us. Hudson pointed at their meat loaf.

"Got any more science to share with us on this stuff?" he asked me.

They all laughed.

There are only so many LADYLIKE ways to say it.

I don't smell.

I'm not STINKFUL.

AS ODORS GO, you could find one worse than me.

Great. I'd become the Meat Loaf Master.
"Mrs. Avon wants me to write a story about it now. I never should have mentioned it."

"Let me help you out with that, Jamie," Isabella volunteered, waving Bruntford over to our table before I knew what was happening.

"Hey, why do they serve this when they know we don't like it?" she asked Bruntford bluntly.

"What kind of question is that?" Bruntford asked.

"The kind people answer," Isabella said.

"It's, um, it's **good for you**," Bruntford said. She started sweating a little. I could tell, because it smelled like a lot of people sweating.

"Not if we don't eat it," Isabella said.

"It's delicious," Bruntford said. "Kids like it. Like cake."

Isabella looked around, and Bruntford's eyes scanned the cafeteria with her. It was a scene of **total disgust**.

"Do they?" Isabella asked.

EVEN A ZOMBIE

"It's, um . . ." Bruntford began.

"Yes?"

"Don't be so selfish," Bruntford oinked at us, and stormed off.

"There's the answer," I said.

"What? What's the answer?" Hudson said.

I put on my smartest face. "If somebody won't tell you the reason, the reason is even worse than refusing to give you the reason."

Angeline smiled and nodded. She would never admit it in a million years, but I know that she knew that was kind of smart.

"That's kind of smart," she said, ahead of schedule by about **a million years.**

Angeline, please do me the courtesy of being mean to me on MY SCHEDULE and NOT when it Doesn't suit you.

WAT

yes it makes sense

FRIDAY 20

Dear Dumb Diary,

Today in science, we talked about something called **commensalism**. It's when one species benefits from a relationship that doesn't harm the other. Like, when cows graze, they stir up bugs that birds eat. It helps the birds, and the cows are unaffected.

Then there's **mutualism**, where both species benefit, like how clown fish eat little critters that hurt sea anemones, and the sea anemone's stingers protect the clown fish from predators.

And there's **parasitism**, where only one species benefits and the other is harmed, like a flea living on a dog. (Stinker has had some fleas, but out of embarrassment, they always lie to the other fleas about where they live.)

That BEAGLE? NAH. NOPE. NO WAY. I LiVE oN A DEAD SKUNK'S BUTT BY THE DuMP.

Mrs. Curie decided to ask me to see if I could summarize the lesson, because she thought I wasn't paying attention.

For the record, making a jillion of those little transparent cube things on your notebook doesn't necessarily mean that you aren't paying attention.

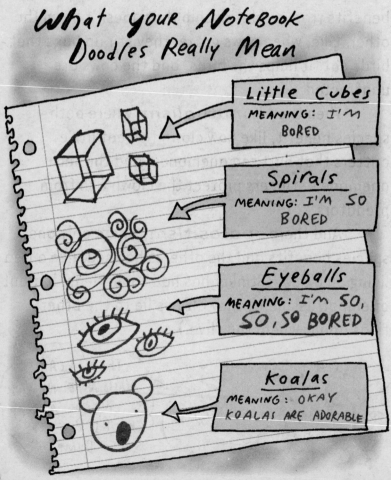

What Your Notebook Doodles Really Mean

Little Cubes
MEANING: I'M BORED

Spirals
MEANING: I'M SO BORED

Eyeballs
MEANING: I'M SO, SO, SO BORED

Koalas
MEANING: OKAY KOALAS ARE ADORABLE

I said that, evidently, nature is always coming up with a new way for somebody to get **messed with**, and that's the main thing I think we need to understand about these relationships.

She said that nobody gets messed with in commensalism or mutualism, and I said that I thought the bugs that the birds eat might **disagree** with her. And the sea anemones are keeping some other animal from enjoying a nice clown fish dinner. And the clown fish is keeping other critters from helping themselves to some delicious anemone. (I just assume they're delicious because they look so much like gummy worms.)

The Great Circle of Everybody messing each other up

"Nope," I said. "All of nature is designed so that we're all messing with each other. All the time. And no matter how perfectly an animal adapts, something is right there to mess with them."

Nobody said anything, so I went on. "You might think, when you look out there at all the trees and flowers and squirrels, that they're in perfect harmony, but they're not. They're locked in a battle that none of them seems to be able to win. They all want what they want, and they don't much care what they have to do to get it." I was on a roll now. **Take that, smartness.** "Those beautiful flowers get water and nutrients from the soil, and they use the sun to create energy, but if they had little mouths and claws, those flowers would **eat us.**"

I had been pointing and looking out the window as I spoke, and I suddenly realized that the room had become silent.

just for example, perhaps they would choose Angeline first.

Mrs. Curie was just staring at me. She seemed to really be processing what I had said.

In fact, everybody was just staring at me. Yolanda looked like she might cry. (Nature is no place for the dainty.)

Finally, Isabella broke the silence.

"YOU GOT THAT RIGHT, GIRLFREN," she said loudly, dropping the *D* on *girlfriend* because it sounds cooler that way.

"Class dismissed," said Mrs. Curie quietly.

SAY EVERYTHING THE COOL WAY

REGULAR WAY	THE COOL WAY
"Hello. How are you?"	"S'up."
"I wish to be truthful and authentic."	"Keepin' it real."
"Look. There's Angeline."	"That girl stole our television."
"Angeline needs help."	"Nice day, isn't it?"
"I have to go do something smart."	"Later."

SATURDAY 21

Dear Dumb Diary,

I worked on my news story for Mrs. Avon today, and even asked Dad for help.

I don't really like asking for help, because it's sort of like admitting I can't do something, but lately I've been thinking that if I have to pound a nail, I don't use my fist, I call upon Mr. Hammer for help. It's easier for me to ask for help when I think of my dad as a **giant tool**.

I told him about the meat loaf questions and how now I had to write about meat loaf for Language Arts.

Hey Dad, can I AXE you a question?

Just kidding — only my DAD is a tool

"Hmmm, I don't know, Jamie. Ask your mom. As you know, she occasionally **commits a meat loaf**. Maybe she'll tell you exactly what's going on there," Dad said, effectively reminding me that sometimes Mr. Hammer bends the nail you've asked him to help you with, and you have to call on Mrs. Pliers to help you pull it out.

Mom was in the kitchen, trying to get Stinker and Stinkette to eat leftovers from last night. (Not a chance.)

I told her all about my story, and she picked up her purse.

"Get in the car."

Mom generously sharing some leftovers with Stinker

enjoy!

SHOVE
CRAM
SHOVE

The next thing I knew, we were in the supermarket.

"Here," Mom said, handing me some cash. "Pick out what we're having for dinner."

I haven't been given this opportunity since The Great Chocolate-Chip Soup scandal of three years ago.

After looking around a little, I came back to the cart.

"This isn't enough money," I said. "I can't get what I want with this."

Mom laughed.

"Welcome to the world," she said.

I knew that I was supposed to learn something, so I popped my eyes open wide and nodded as I pointed at Mom and laughed a little.

I have no idea how the grocery-store trip was supposed to help me with Language Arts, but I knew how to make it come to an end.

AH HAH

This makes the Lesson end.

SUNDAY 22

Dear Dumb Diary,

Isabella and I got calls from both the Camera Club and the Running Club to bring in something for the fund-raising bake sales they're doing tomorrow.

I told her that I'm afraid if we don't participate, they'll start asking questions about our commitment and this will lead to us being kicked out of the clubs. Pretty soon, questions will be asked about all of these clubs we joined and the next thing you know, my future will be destroyed and Isabella will be still living with her mean older brothers when she's 75.

It was that **last part** that got through to Isabella.

"Just bring some money and a paper plate," she said.

I sabella will be **SUCH** A cute old Lady!

Except when she's swearing at Butterflies and disturbing OLD LADY stuff like that.

MONDAY 23

Dear Dumb Diary,

Today, I gave Isabella my money and she bought a whole plate of brownies from the Camera Club bake sale. She put half of them on the paper plate, and we walked down the hall to where they were having the Running Club bake sale.

"Here's our contribution," she said with a **big lying smile**.

Then we went around the corner, where she took out the bag of coffee and sprinkled some on the brownies we had kept.

"Let's go," she said, and I tagged along cluelessly as she started knocking on classroom doors.

"Anybody interested in some coffee-flavored brownies?" she asked. "Mocha-java brownies! Fund-raiser for the Camera Club!" she crowed.

That was all the teachers had to hear in order to pull out their wallets and happily give us four times what we'd paid for the brownies in the first place.

NORMAL SMILE → (◡) (◡) ← Lying smile

Then we walked back to the Running Club bake sale with the money and bought a plate of cookies. We took **those** back to the Camera Club bake sale.

"Here's our contribution," Isabella said with another big lying smile, and we walked away.

Isabella turned to me. "That's how we do it."

"Great," I said. "But it still cost me money."

"No, it didn't," she said. "We have some cash left over." She handed me what we had left. I actually made a dollar on the deal.

I think it's now **pretty clear** what Isabella is going to be when she grows up.

I used to think she was going to be the Devil. Now I think she's going to be the Devil's mean boss who he complains about to Mrs. Devil every evening after work.

On the way out of school, we signed up for the Dance Club, and watched them dance for a few minutes.

I think we were considering actually attending this one, but the way that they dance really isn't compatible with the way Isabella dances, what with them all dancing to the beat and being good at dancing.

We signed up anyway, and now with **eight** extracurricular clubs, plus the one we created, plus soccer, I can feel the colleges just begging me to attend them now.

TUESDAY 24

Dear Dumb Diary,

    Mrs. Curie seemed rattled in class today. She almost fell asleep at her desk.

    On the way out, I asked her if everything was okay, and she said she had been thinking about what I said about nature **messing with people**.

    She said that those animals didn't think about the results of their actions.

    "Maybe the clown fish never thought about the little critters she was eating," she whispered. "Maybe the clown fish didn't think that her actions might result in them eating meat loaf."

"Oh my gosh," I said. Mrs. Curie looked more upset than she should be by clown fish.

I tried my best to make her feel better.

"There's a pretty good chance that you are insane," I said **sweetly**. "Let's go down to the office and see if they have one of those cold things to put on your head."

We walked down to the office together. You remember, Dumb Diary, that my Aunt Carol works there, which is good because she's super-nice and I suspect that the insane find that comforting.

"Aunt Carol," I said in a very nurse-like way, "could you please talk to Mrs. Curie here? She's not feeling well. She may have **lost her mind**, but I don't feel that I'm fully qualified to diagnose that."

I left the office feeling pretty good, and I'm confident that if I wanted to, I could be a doctor when I grow up, or a person that handles sweet old donkeys that have gone bonkers.

I have to go now, DD, and finish my Language Arts homework.

WEDNESDAY 25

Dear Dumb Diary,

I stopped by the office today to ask Aunt Carol about Mrs. Curie. Aunt Carol said she was fine, and that she had been suffering with a headache and needed to talk to Uncle Dan. She had left school a little early yesterday and took today off.

I had to turn in that headline and news article today to Mrs. Avon.

I never really did answer my own question. All I could do was kind of build on it a little. Maybe I *am* the dumb one. Anyway, here's what I came up with:

MEAT LOAF. NOBODY LIKES IT.
WHY IS IT SERVED?

When you ask this question around the school, you'll get answers here and there, but none of them seem correct. And the people who probably do know why absolutely refuse to give you any answer at all. Something doesn't smell right here, and it's not just the cafeteria every Thursday.

Mrs. Avon read my article out loud to the class. They nodded in agreement, and then they asked me why I thought I couldn't get an answer. Mrs. Avon smiled at me with even more gum than usual. I'd say, like, **35% more**.

"Excellent work, Jamie," she said.

"But I didn't even answer the question," I said.

She motioned around the room at the other kids.

"No, but look at your readership. They want to know more. They might even **demand** to know more. Sometimes all you have to do is flip on the lights, Jamie. You don't have the answer, but I think you have a lot more people interested if you ever do find it."

Maybe sometimes journalism is about the questions.

CORN OIL is made of corn. What's BABY OIL made of?

How do we know there's an infinity? Has anybody ever counted up to it to check?

PAIR OF PANTS? Is there such a thing as ONE PANT? How would you wear it?

THURSDAY 26

Dear Dumb Diary,

Isabella and I got called down to the office before lunch. I started to freak out just a little on the way.

"We're busted," I whispered. "We're so busted. The extracurriculars. The Permanent Records. The *coffee*."

Isabella looked at me calmly. Her mouth was as straight and thin as a paper cut.

"Don't lose it on me, Jamie," she said. **"Be calm."**

"You're going to have to live at home with your brothers forever," I said, encouraging her to join me in the freak-out.

She stopped and grabbed me by the collar.

"I will kung fu my way out of that office, take you as a hostage, and jump a train to Mexico before that happens, Jamie."

Oh, Isabella. If had a nickel for every time you made that threat.

Lovely girl smothered in nickels

When we got to the office, we were pretty surprised to find that Bruntford, Mrs. Curie, and Angeline were all sitting there with Uncle Dan. He looked more principally than I have ever seen him, and he had our Permanent Records on his desk.

Oh boy.

"So," he began. "It looks like you two have been pretty busy."

"You mean like with cleaning our rooms and doing homework and being good and helping the poor and doing our homework?" I stammered nervously. Isabella put her hand on my knee and squeezed it hard enough to leave a bruise.

"What do you mean, '*You've been busy*'?" she asked calmly.

"Jamie, you've signed up for eight extracurriculars in three weeks? Plus, you're doing soccer?" Uncle Dan said.

Isabella nodded. "That's right," she said.

"Jamie," he said, holding up a copy of the article I wrote for Mrs. Avon's class, "tell me about the meat loaf."

Isabella answered before I could say anything.

"The meat loaf they serve here is awful. We all hate it."

Angeline nodded.

"Isabella, if you don't mind, I'd like to hear it from Jamie."

I swallowed hard.

"It's just like it says there. Nobody likes it, but the school serves it to us every Thursday and they always have. Maybe I'm dumb, but that makes no sense to me," I said.

Maybe Isabella is going to be a LION TAMER?

"At your suggestion, I finally tried that meat loaf," Uncle Dan said. "You're not dumb, Jamie, not by a long shot. That stuff is horrible. And I looked into it. Mrs. Bruntford, could you please explain?"

And then it all came out.

Actually, there wasn't a lot to come out.

Here's the **BIG SECRET**: It's cheap. That's pretty much it. The meat loaf they use is cheap.

If that had been the end of it, I would have understood. Mom has to buy cheap stuff all the time. It's like Miss Anderson said at the Cuisine Club: You have to keep your meals on a budget and not overspend on one item . . .

. . . or you won't have any money for anything else.

I wonder if this was what Mom was teaching me at the grocery store while I wasn't learning.

PLEASE DO NOT PUT NORMAL MEAT INTO THE LOAFER

"Now, Jamie. Could you please tell us about **the coffee**?" Uncle Dan asked suddenly, and I started to twitch.

Isabella jumped to her feet.

"You ever meet my brothers?" she hissed. "It's not going to go down this way. Which way is Mexico?"

Angeline smiled at me, and for some reason I calmed down. **Angeline knew something.**

I put my hand on Isabella's arm and slowly guided her back to her chair. She was about ten seconds from foaming up.

"Which coffee?" I asked.

"The coffee that the teachers serve in the Teachers' Lounge," Uncle Dan said.

"Well, it's really good coffee," I said simply.

Isabella was getting a little kidnappy.

"It's really, really good coffee. *Really* good coffee. The kind that costs a lot, I bet," Uncle Dan agreed.

Then Bruntford explained how they could afford it.

They've been saving money on the meat loaf and using it to buy great coffee for the Teachers' Lounge.

Bruntford has been doing it for a few years now because she thought the teachers deserved it, and Mrs. Curie was the one helping her keep the Teachers' Lounge supplied. Mrs. Curie looked like she wanted to cry while she explained.

"Jamie, I thought it was commensalism. You know, the way the cows stir up bugs for the birds. I didn't think it harmed anything. But I realize now that I hadn't thought about the bugs. You made me see that."

"So, let's toss these old hags in jail, **am I right?**" Isabella said to Uncle Dan, quickly regaining her composure and wiping a small amount of foam from her lips.

They are so Lucky that Isabella

Didn't have her handcuffs with her.

"Hang on a second. There **is** the matter of signing up for all these clubs," Uncle Dan said.

"They were trying to figure out what was going on with the coffee," Angeline jumped in. "As you all know, I'm the one that gets all of the extracurricular sign-up information from the clubs, and I give it all to our assistant principal here."

OH MY GOSH. THAT'S HOW ANGELINE KNEW WHAT WE WERE SIGNING UP FOR.

"And I think it's pretty obvious that Jamie and Isabella have been trying to figure this out for a while."

Assistant Principal Uncle Dan looked at her with some disbelief.

"Jamie took up chess to form a strategy. They needed to learn about cameras in case she needed photo evidence, so they joined the Camera Club. The Agricultural Club taught them about beef and coffee, and she joined that Organization Club because there was a lot to keep straight."

"Uh-huh. What about the Running Club? The Videogamer Club?" Uncle Dan asked, flipping through our folders. He looked **unconvinced**.

Isabella decided to help explain.

"The Running Club was so we'd have an excuse for being late while we acquired the coffee sample," Isabella said. "And the Videogamer Club was so we'd have some nerds to use as human shields if this got ugly."

"No. Not that last part," I said. "We weren't going to use human shields."

Uncle Dan stared at us for a minute. "The Dance Club? The Cuisine Club?"

"The Cuisine Club! Yeah, that's the best part," Angeline said. "Jamie and Isabella were hoping we could all have lunch together today."

I'm a little concerned that now Bruntford is aware of the DANCE CLUB

something like this could make Humanity stop making music.

It wasn't something you see every day: Bruntford, Uncle Dan, Mrs. Curie, and Miss Anderson sat down to a meat loaf lunch with Angeline, Isabella, Hudson, and me.

We talked about the price of things, and Miss Anderson asked a lot of questions about the food service that provides the meat loaf. She went through some of the ordering information that Bruntford had brought along and demonstrated how, with a little imagination and artistry, we could come up with alternatives that the kids would like better, and wouldn't cost any more than meat loaf.

That's right, Dumb Diary. And you know who was doing all of the math on this? **ME.**

"There's still enough left over for the teachers to have their fancy coffee," I said. "And I think we should let them have it. It's not a big deal, and they sure seem to like it. They weren't really doing anything **wrong**, they just hadn't thought it through."

"As the secretary of the Student Awareness Committee, I second that motion," Angeline said, reminding me of how much I hate it when people talk like that.

"What's the Student Awareness Committee?" Uncle Dan asked.

"It's the extracurricular that Jamie and I started," Isabella said. "It's the organization that cracked this whole crime ring."

"Does it have a teacher sponsor?" he asked.

"It sure does," Mrs. Curie said. I could hardly believe that she volunteered to do it, after our little difficulties. It gives me hope that maybe one day an anemone will gallantly turn off his stingers, and let some poor hungry creature just eat that clown fish for once.

"Jamie is the president," Angeline added. "You have all the paperwork on your desk."

And then, just like that, Mrs. Curie and I were okay. Plus, now Isabella and I have this awesome thing in our Permanent Records, and nobody thinks of me as **the dumb one** anymore.

And for the first time ever, I actually finished the school meat loaf without complaining. It's the last time they'll ever serve it, and I can honestly say, it's **never tasted better**.

FRIDAY 27

Dear Dumb Diary,

    We had our field trip to the science museum today. For some reason, looking out the window of the bus and watching the road go by helped me think.

    I think I'm actually going to go to the Cuisine Club, and maybe even the Running Club. (It's pretty clear that I need to exercise.) Isabella said she's going to go to the Videogamer Club. She wants to secretly get good at games so she can beat her older brothers while pretending it was the first time she ever played. And she's making Angeline go, too, so she won't be the only girl.

    As the bus bumped along, I thought about my future — my **perfect** future. And I thought about everybody else's future.

Future me
(that's right:
I invented the
FLYING
ROBOT COUCH)

Angeline can be whatever she wants, of course, but not because she's so horribly pretty. Angeline is smart and thoughtful and really comes through for you even though you don't want to be in debt to her. I forgave her for lying about Hudson and the coffee. She was just mad that I had excluded her. She'll probably be president one day, and I'll vote for her. Of course, I'll tell her I voted for the other guy. Angeline, out of pity, probably actually **will** vote for her opponent.

Yolanda will do something dainty, like be a brain surgeon or knit sweaters for mosquitoes that have to live in colder climates.

Also teensy socks

Hudson won't have to work. I'll make enough so that he can stay home and watch our perfect kids, Michelangelo, Geronimo, and Caramel. I'm not sure about **all** those names, of course. I might not go with Michelangelo.

I looked over at Isabella, my best friend, and even though she'd said it was obvious, I **STILL** had no idea what she was going to be one day.

She had enough of the special teacher coffee left over to make herself just one single cup, and she had it with her in a thermos. As she was opening it, she spilled it on Hudson.

The smell, along with the bus ride, made him throw up. But like I said before, it's a school bus so nobody cared. Free pass.

I watched Isabella fearlessly clean up the barf with a couple of sheets of notebook paper. There was something about how she was laughing the whole time that made it all clear to me.

Isabella is clever and quick and dangerous when she needs to be. She will mess you up in one second, but she's always been there for me, even when it was just to yell at me. She's very difficult to fool, and I just can't help but like her, even when I don't.

totally not grossed out by grossness →

"Isabella," I whispered. "I know what you're going to be one day."

Isabella smiled and flipped the gross, wadded-up notebook paper at me and I ducked.

"Of course you do, Jamie. You're all smart like that."

"You're going to be a **teacher**," I said confidently.

"A perfect one," she added.

"As close as it gets, anyway," I said, you know, all smart like that.

Thanks for listening, Dumb Diary,

Jamie Kelly

What's Your Future?

Okay, you know your life is going to be totally perfect. But you can find out more about what the future has in store by answering these questions!

1.) If you forgot to study for a test, what would you do?
   a. Point out to the teacher that tests aren't really a true measure of how much we know.
   b. Fake a horrible disease and go to the nurse's office.
   c. Release bag of bats in classroom (requires some preparation).

2.) Of these choices, which is your favorite school
subject?
a. Art
b. Math
c. Lunch

3.) On a Sunday afternoon, what are you usually doing?
a. Homework that I put off until the very last
minute.
b. Anything I want! I finished my homework on
Friday night.
c. Waiting for my dad to fall asleep on the couch
so I can change the TV channel from football
to a glorious dance movie.

4.) What animal are you most like?
a. A cute and big-eyed koala
b. A noble horse
c. A friendly dolphin that is also part koala on
his mom's side

5.) How many extracurricular activities are you
involved in?
a. 1–2
b. 5+
c. 3–4

6.) If your stinky beagle or other doglike pet was foaming at the mouth, what would you do?

a. My stinky beagle is always foaming at the mouth. Foam is how he communicates. How is this different than any other time?

b. Call the vet right away. (It's not rabies. Rabies would choose a cuter dog.)

c. Check to make sure he didn't eat a whole tube of toothpaste (which is likely).

7.) Of these choices, what's your favorite color?

a. Sparkle colored

b. A nice, calming blue

c. Purple

If you answered . . .

Mostly As: You have an artistic future ahead of you! Or maybe not. No matter what you end up doing, you'll do it with creativity, flair, and a smirk on your face.

Mostly Bs: You're orderly and like things just so, and you have organizational skills that will get you far. Except for that disaster you call a bedroom. Weren't you supposed to clean your room? Oh, and about your future: It's going to rock.

Mostly Cs: You will probably be good at anything you want to do. You may even be good things you don't want to do.

HEY! WHATEVER YOU DO, DON'T LOOK FOR JAMIE KELLY'S NEXT **TOP SECRET** DIARY....

DEAR DUMB DIARY YEAR TWO #4:
WHAT I DON'T KNOW MIGHT HURT ME

Turn the page for a super-secret sneak peek. . . .

#1: Let's Pretend This Never Happened

#2: My Pants Are Haunted!

#3: Am I the Princess or the Frog?

#4: Never Do Anything, Ever

#5: Can Adults Become Human?

#6: The Problem With Here Is That It's Where I'm From

#7: Never Underestimate Your Dumbness

#8: It's Not My Fault I Know Everything

#9: That's What Friends Aren't For

#10: The Worst Things In Life Are Also Free

#11: Okay, So Maybe I Do Have Superpowers

#12: Me! (Just Like You, Only Better)

Our Dumb Diary: A Journal to Share

Totally Not Boring School Planner

read them all!

Life, Starring Me!

Callie for President

Drama Queen

I've Got a Secret

Confessions of a Bitter Secret Santa

Super Sweet 13

The Boy Next Door

The Sister Switch

Snowfall Surprise

Rumor Has It

The Sweetheart Deal

The Accidental Cheerleader

The Babysitting Wars

Star-Crossed

Accidentally
Fabulous

Accidentally
Famous

Accidentally
Fooled

Accidentally
Friends

How to Be a Girly Girl in
Just Ten Days

Ice Dreams

Juicy Gossip

Making Waves

Miss Popularity

Miss Popularity
Goes Camping

Miss Popularity
and the Best Friend Disaster

Totally Crushed

Wish You Were Here,
Liza

See You Soon,
Samantha

Miss You, Mina

Winner Takes All

POISON APPLE BOOKS

The Dead End

This Totally Bites!

Miss Fortune

Now You See Me...

Midnight Howl

Her Evil Twin

Curiosity Killed the Cat

At First Bite

THRILLING.

BONE-CHILLING

THESE BOOKS

HAVE BITE!

Danny Shine just wants to draw comics.
But first, he has to get his name off of

THE LOSER LIST

Read them all!

About Jim Benton

Jim Benton is not a middle-school girl, but do not hold that against him. He has managed to make a living out of being funny, anyway.

He is the creator of many licensed properties, some for big kids, some for little kids, and some for grown-ups who, frankly, are probably behaving like little kids.

You may already know his properties: It's Happy Bunny™ or Just Jimmy™, and of course you already know about Dear Dumb Diary.

He's created a kids' TV series, designed clothing, and written books.

Jim Benton lives in Michigan with his spectacular wife and kids. They do not have a dog, and they especially do not have a vengeful beagle. This is his first series for Scholastic.

Jamie Kelly has no idea that Jim Benton, or you, or anybody is reading her diaries. So, please, please, please don't tell her.